RodersMagnet, LLC

Nobody is Somebody
Copyright © 2022 by *Dr. Sandra C. Birchfield*. All rights reserved.

Published in the United States of America.
ISBN   Paperback: 978-1-956780-59-8
ISBN   eBook: 978-1-956780-58-1

All rights reserved. No part of this publication may be reproduced, stored in a retrieval system or transmitted in any way by any means, electronic, mechanical, photocopy, recording or otherwise without the prior permission of the author except as provided by USA copyright law.

The opinions expressed by the author are not necessarily those of ReadersMagnet, LLC.

ReadersMagnet, LLC
10620 Treena Street, Suite 230 | San Diego, California, 92131 USA
1.619. 354. 2643 | www.readersmagnet.com

Book design copyright © 2022 by ReadersMagnet, LLC. All rights reserved.
Cover design by Ericka Obando
Interior design by Mary Mae Romero

For my grandchildren Levi, Benjamin, Josie, and Sophie

Take note to the "nobodies" of the world!

"nobody is SOMEBODY"

There was once a boy named "nobody"

He lived in a small house with "Everybody"

Children teased him and made fun

Called him names, but he would not run.

One day while going through a drawer
He found something that made him fall to the floor
"nobody" had been looking for his favorite toy,
When he found special papers for a little boy.

Adoption papers was it what it seemed?

Was this real or just a dream?

"We should have told you" as Mom and Dad began to talk

"Before we knew it you could walk".

All our love we give to you day and night

We treated you well and did what was right

We did not tell you, we were wrong,

You were one of us and this is where you belong.

"nobody" decided to go to the gym and play

It was not his favorite place to stay

He felt as if he had not been trained

He liked games and puzzles, things that teased the brain.

One day nobody went outside to play

The coach was there and he heard him say

"Hey nobody let's play some ball"

"nobody" wanted nothing to do with that at all.

"nobody" was not sure what to do, but he gave it

His all

He watched, listened, and tried hard to hit the ball

It was not the greatest hit he had ever done

But he had to admit it was fun.

There were those who did not follow the plan

They never seemed to understand

"nobody" bothered "No one"

"No one" bothered "Someone"

"Someone" bothered "Somebody"

"Somebody" bothered "Everybody".

One day the school received word that they would be

Selected as the site for the "Spelling Bee."

The names of each spellers were filed

A list of words was given to each child.

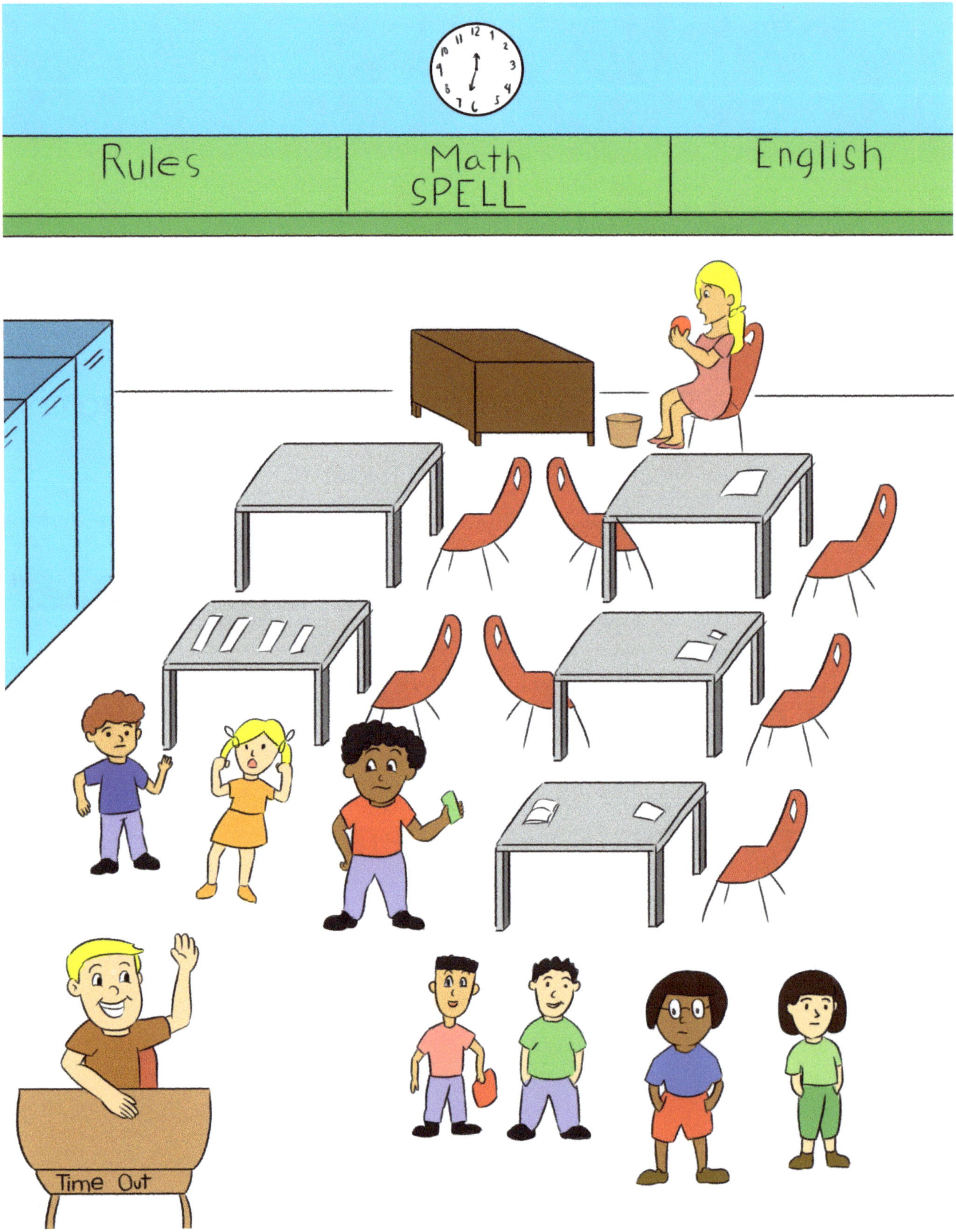
Rules
Math
SPELL
English
Time Out

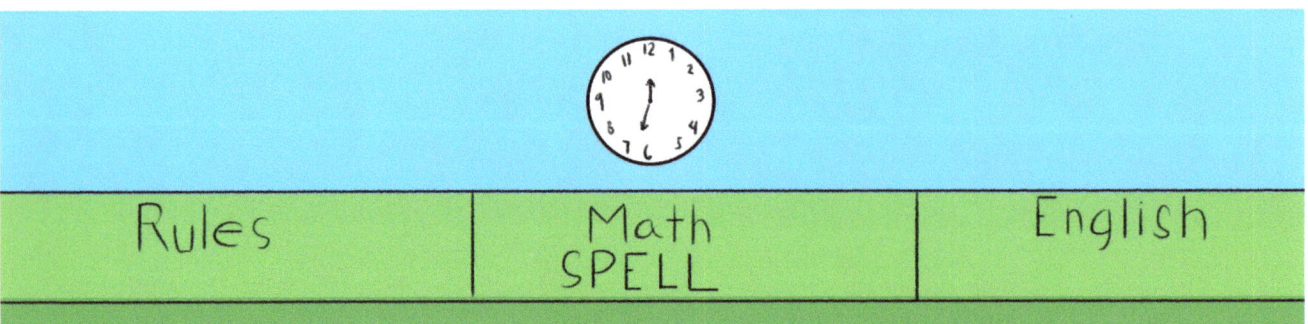

"nobody" wanted to participate and to help his school

"nobody" always finished what he started

He did not like to be outsmarted

He talked to the counselor, added his name, and competed

No one, Someone, Somebody, and Everybody could not believe it.

"nobody" became "SOMEBODY" as he spelled word after word

The news around town was "Have you heard?"

Students gave "NOBODY" their words of praise

The louder shouts of cheer were raised.

"NOBODY" had found what must be done

Put into practice what you have learned

This story is real and you know it is true

How "nobody" becomes a "SOMEBODY" is up to you.

Look around as you go your way

It is simple as it can be

Each day three little words you need to say

"Just be Me".

SAY IT AND YOU WILL "SEE"

10620 Treena Street, Suite 230

San Diego, California,

CA 92131 USA

www.readersmagnet.com

1.619.354.2643

Copyright 2022 All Rights Reserved

www.ingramcontent.com/pod-product-compliance
Lightning Source LLC
LaVergne TN
LVHW070219080526
838202LV00067B/6859